W9-BAG-790

# WELCOME TO
# PASSPORT TO READING
## A beginning reader's ticket to a brand-new world!

Every book in this program is designed to build read-along and read-alone skills, level by level, through engaging and enriching stories. As the reader turns each page, he or she will become more confident with new vocabulary, sight words, and comprehension.

These PASSPORT TO READING levels will help you choose the perfect book for every reader.

### READING TOGETHER
Read short words in simple sentence structures together to begin a reader's journey.

### READING OUT LOUD
Encourage developing readers to sound out words in more complex stories with simple vocabulary.

### READING INDEPENDENTLY
Newly independent readers gain confidence reading more complex sentences with higher word counts.

### READY TO READ MORE
Readers prepare for chapter books with fewer illustrations and longer paragraphs.

This book features sight words from the educator-supported Dolch Sight Word List. Readers will become more familiar with these commonly used vocabulary words, increasing reading speed and fluency.

For more information, please visit www.passporttoreadingbooks.com, where each reader can add stamps to a personalized passport while traveling through story after story!

*Enjoy the journey!*

# LAIKA

Little, Brown and Company

Hachette Book Group
237 Park Avenue, New York, NY 10017
Visit our website at www.lb-kids.com

Little, Brown and Company is a division of Hachette Book Group, Inc.
The Little, Brown name and logo are trademarks of
Hachette Book Group, Inc.

The publisher is not responsible for websites (or their content)
that are not owned by the publisher.

First Edition: July 2012

ISBN 978-0-316-20982-3

10 9 8 7 6 5 4 3 2

CW

Printed in the United States of America

# PARANORMAN

## Meet the Ghosts

Adapted by Lucy Rosen

Based on the animated feature screenplay
by Chris Butler

LITTLE, BROWN AND COMPANY
New York  Boston

Attention, *ParaNorman* fans!
Can you find these items in this book?

house

soldier

hippie

graveyard

Meet Norman.

Norman lives in a regular house
with a regular family.
Everything about him
seems perfectly, well, normal.

Except for one little thing.
Norman can talk to ghosts,
such as his grandma.

"Grandma says it is cold
and to turn on the heat," says Norman.
"Your grandmother is gone, son,"
Norman's dad says.

"I know you miss her,"
says Norman's mom,
"but Grandma is in a better place."
"No, she is not," says Norman.
"She is in the living room."

No one believes
in Norman's special gift.
Not his parents, not his sister,
and definitely not the kids at school.

"Hey, Norman," says Alvin,
the biggest bully in school.
He swats a fly with his hand.
"Try talking to *that*."
"Flies do not talk," Norman mutters.

Norman sees ghosts
everywhere he looks.
"Peace, man," a hippie ghost calls out
as Norman walks to school.
"Totally," Norman calls back.

"Morning, Mrs. Hardman.
You look nice today,"
says Norman as he runs past
a lady ghost.

"Hey, little buddy," Norman coos
to a dead raccoon.
A passerby stops and stares.
"Whoops," says Norman.
He hurries away, embarrassed.

Then Norman passes
a soldier ghost and salutes.
"As you were," says the soldier,
and salutes back.
Norman relaxes but notices that
everyone is now staring at him.

Not everyone in town
thinks Norman is strange.
Norman has a friend named Neil.

Neil invites Norman over
to play with his dog, Bub.
Bub is a ghost!

"This is great," says Neil. "We can play with the dog, and we do not even have to dig him up first!"

Neil pets the air.

"Bub cannot play fetch anymore,
you know," says Norman.
"It is still fun," says Neil,
catching the stick himself.

Norman knows he has a friend, but he still feels pretty lonely. It is hard being the only one who can see and talk to ghosts.

But Norman does not know
that there is one ghost
who is looking for him.

One day in school,
a ghost appears to Norman.
He is the creepy man
who lived in a house by the graveyard.

"I know what you see,"
the ghost tells Norman.
"This town is cursed,
and you are the only
one who can save it!"
*"Me?"* asks Norman.

"Yes, you," says the ghost.
"Long ago, a witch cast a spell.
You have to use your gift
to keep this town safe."

"How?" asks Norman.

"You have to talk to the witch!
Watch for the signs," explains the ghost.

"You will know what to do."

Then the ghost vanishes!

Later that day,

the sky turns a strange color.

Clouds swirl as the wind

starts to howl through the trees.

"The witch is coming!"

Norman gasps.

He runs home.

Norman is scared.

He is just a boy.

How can he get an evil witch

to break her curse?

"There is nothing wrong with being scared," says Norman's grandmother. "Just do not let it change who you are."

Norman thinks.
Maybe there is a reason
why he is special.
He is the only one
who can save the town!

Outside, the sky deepens
into a green color.
Norman knows the witch is near.
He has no time to lose.

Norman goes to the graveyard. He is ready to face the witch the only way he knows how— by just being himself.